THE NO-NAME MAN OF THE MOUNTAIN

The No-Name Man of the Mountain

WILLIAM O. STEELE

Illustrated by Jack Davis

Harcourt, Brace & World, Inc., New York

THE NO-NAME MAN OF THE MOUNTAIN

Chapter 1

There were once three brothers who lived way back among the high hills of Tennessee. The two oldest were twins and answered to the names of Creel and Huckabuck. The youngest brother had no name at all, but he did have a farm on top of the highest mountain in Tennessee.

The twins had given him this land, and he was mighty proud of it. He didn't mind a-tall that he didn't have a name because his brothers had taken it away from him for safe-keeping. They said the air on his mountaintop was so terribly thin that a good name such as his wouldn't last long. It would just waste away.

It showed what kind, thoughty brothers Creel and Huckabuck were. Every day younger brother thanked his lucky stars for the twins and the care they took of him. They were the oldest, and he was sure they knew what was best for him.

Younger brother didn't even mind wearing a sack over his head, for he knew he was as ugly as a mud fence. The twins had told him that. It was an onion sack, and the inside smelled so pleasant and friendly that younger brother couldn't help but like it.

O N I O N was printed across the front of the sack. Creel had cut out the two O's for younger brother to use as eyeholes, and this worked fine. The corners of the sack stuck up like the ears of a great horned owl. This tickled younger brother mightily. He wore the onion sack over his head day and night, through chilblains and storms and the dog days of summer. Even after the last thunder of winter had brought out the snakes and the good weather, younger brother kept the covering over his face.

Creel said younger brother was so ugly that once when he washed in the river, the water turned sour and the uglies had to be skimmed off the river every day for weeks thereafter. Huckabuck remembered the time younger brother walked past a pond where a dozen decoy ducks floated. One glance at his ugly face scared those wooden ducks so bad that they flew away from the pond and never came back.

Younger brother believed them. One time with the sack off, he had tried to sneak up on a mirror from behind. Before he could even get around in front of it, the mirror shattered to pieces.

On his mountain farm, younger brother had five chickens, four hogs, and two black-spotted milk cows, one with a wilted horn. He had built all his animals fine places in which to live. But he hadn't been quite so clever at making his own house.

He had never in his whole life built a log cabin. Yet he wanted one the worse way, so he set to work. He cut down a heap of trees and used their green trunks for the walls. When the sap dried out of those logs, they warped and buckled to a fare-thee-well and ended up twisted about most nigh every which way.

There were such big gaps and holes in the four walls that younger brother had more outside in his cabin than there was in the yard. Those holes were so big that geese migrating north in the springtime often flew through his walls.

And the roof—great ragged buzzards! The trouble it gave younger brother. He had no idea what to cover his cabin with. He finally mixed up a huge batch of biscuit dough and spread it all around smooth and even over the top of the cabin. The first time the warm sunlight hit that biscuit dough, it began to rise. It rose higher and higher and swelled up bigger and bigger and bigger.

9

The last younger brother saw of his roof, it was a-flying off into the sunset. Caught fast on one side of it was his good stone chimney, still smoking from a fire under a pot of beans cooking on the hearth.

One spring day younger brother noticed that his farm was terribly crowded and way too small. His farm was so small, there wasn't enough air to go around at one time. He and his stock had to take turns breathing. The pigs breathed while younger brother and the chickens and cows held their breaths. Then it was the chickens' turn to use the air while all the others held their breaths. And so on around till everybody had a chance to suck in a chestful.

The farm was so crowded that when younger brother milked the cows, there was no place to put the bucket. Crowded! Great day in the morning, it was so crowded that it took *only* four eggs to make a dozen. Whenever younger brother planted turnips and turned around at the end of the row, two beets in the next row had to hold on to each other to stay in their proper furrow.

At last younger brother decided it was time he told Creel and Huckabuck about his troubles. He hated to be a bother to them. Howsomever, he couldn't stand being crowded any longer. He trimmed his toenails in a neat and proper fashion, brushed the dirt from his onion sack, and headed off down the mountain.

There was only one way to leave the farm, and that was

down a narrow valley that ended up right smack behind the twins' cabin. But it wasn't easy to get through the valley. Younger brother had to fight every step of the way. Why, the sides of that valley were so close together, it would take two men to hunt in it—one man to fire at the game, while the other man ran ahead and held back the valley's walls so the bullet could get through.

When younger brother finally reached the lower end of the valley, he found it closed good and tight. The sides had been stitched together with rope and bailing wire and well chains. Planks had been nailed across all the holes. He peeked out through a crack. On trees and bushes about the valley entrance, all manner of warnings and contagious signs had been stuck up.

BEWARE!
POISON COW CROSSING

RUN! DANGER!
MEASLES SPOTTED HERE

QUARANTINE
BAD CASE OF
PAVEMENT NARROWS

It brought a sob to younger brother's lips to see all the trouble the twins had taken just to try to protect him. He appreciated all their work. The signs were beautiful. Never had there been brothers with such kind ways and sweet intentions as his two older brothers.

A tear swelled up in his eye and trickled down his nose. He snuffled a time or two. He didn't deserve such brothers. Then, clearing his throat, he yelled.

Creel and Huckabuck came running out of their cabin at once and right up to the closed-tight valley. They wanted to know what ailed younger brother. He told them that his farm was no good and it was too small and a heap too crowded for him to stay there any longer.

Creel scolded younger brother. "You ought to be ashamed of yourself," he hollered through the boarded-up entrance. "It ain't everybody nor their spitting kin who can own a farm as good as that one of yours. Why, me and Creel have done everything we can to give you the very best and to make it easy for you. And this is the thanks we get for our trouble."

Inside the valley, younger brother hung his head. He had caused the twins terrible pain and sorrow. It was more than he could bear.

"Now," Huckabuck said sternly to younger brother, "I want to point out that you not only have a rip-dandy mountaintop to farm, but you got all the four sides below it. Why, me and Creel ain't got but this one bitsy dab of flat ground here at the end of this valley. It can't hold a candle to that fine farm of yours."

Younger brother felt lower than a crawdad at the bottom of a well. He was ashamed that he had spoken out. What Huckabuck had said was true. He had five pieces of mountaintop to use, though he hadn't discovered it for himself. But if that was the case, then it couldn't be crowded. How silly he was not to have noticed this before now!

He straightened the sack on his head. He'd not complain nary another time. It wasn't brotherly of him. He bade the twins good day and made his way up the valley toward his cabin. He swung along a-figuring what he could do to make the twins proud of him. Finally he reckoned it'd be grand if he cleared off one of the mountainsides below his farm.

He hurried forward, feeling as happy and grand as a katynipper and so pleased with himself that he couldn't stay on the path. He walked a foot or two above it in the air. Warblers in the tall green hazy beeches called down encouragement. Streams arched from rock to rock and sprayed him with cheering drops. It was the best kind of spring day, just right for clearing a field and readying it for planting.

Younger brother no sooner reached his farm than he

snatched up his grubbing hoe. He gripped it tight enough to make it squeak. "Look out, weeds!" he shouted. "Look out, hands! Look out, feet!"

Flailing away with the hoe for all he was worth, he ran into his mountainside field. Now this field was the kind that a body stands a better chance of leaning against than of walking across. It was steep, for a fact. That field was so steep that the moment he stepped in it, he fell smack dab out of it.

Down the mountain he tumbled. The grubbing hoe fell too. Both of them smashed into the rocks below with a terrible thump. Dust, trees, startled bears, and one small valley went shooting up in the air. When all settled back into place, there lay the hoe. And there lay younger brother. The hoe was killed dead, but younger brother was not much hurt.

"Tanbark and bullhides!" he roared.

He got up and rushed back up the mountain to his farm. With another hoe he stepped back into that steep field. Whang-a-rang-o! Down he went to the rocks below.

The second fall frumulated his brain. It sizzled his gullet. It ramified both his ears till they glowed red-hot. Still younger brother aimed to clear that field. He got up and looked at the hoe. It was busted to smithereens and was a pitiful sight to see. Shaking his head sadly, he crawled back up to the top.

"No field's going to outsmart me," he muttered. "I may

be ugly as a wagon wheel, but I ain't stupid one bit." *stop*

This time he rolled himself in sand so he wouldn't slide off. He put cockleburs between his toes to stick to the ground. He filled his pockets with heavy rocks. He fetched a third hoe and set to work again to try to chop down the weeds. No sooner did he step into that steep field than he fell off once more.

This time he couldn't get up. He lay among the rocks all bumped and battered. When he finally opened his jaws to moan a few times, his elbow said "Ouch!" He wiggled his big toe and one arm leaped upright, both eyes crossed, and the sack jumped off his head and danced the Highland fling, double time.

"Why, I'm as scrambled up as pullet eggs in a skillet," he thought dismally.

Suddenly a big family of blue-tailed skinks came scooting over the rocks to stand around and stare down at him with cold little hungry eyes. Then they moved up close and poked at his remains. They fell to arguing among themselves about which one of them deserved the drumstick and which the gizzard and which the wing and neck.

That did it! Younger brother pulled himself together and got up out of there, wild and mad as parsley in Virginny. "You can have that hoe carcass," he yelled at the skinks, "but I got more to do than stay here and feed shiftless, un-working lizard critters like you."

15

When he felt more like himself, he trotted down the valley to his brothers' farm. Reaching the barricade, he pounded on the boards. He ranted. He raved. The twins rushed to him. Younger brother told them how hard it was on him to keep falling out of his field. "And it's powerful hard on hoes too," he finished up.

"Ta-la-ra, brother. That field's not steep," Creel assured him.

"I sure thought it was," younger brother said, feeling all of his many bumps and bruises.

They sent him home with an old horse that went by the name of Felkin. Now Felkin had suffered a sad accident through being left in a shed that was too small for him. Half of him had stuck out in the weather, and a terrible rain had shrunk the legs on that side till they were a foot shorter than his inside legs. However, this made him mighty useful on steep mountainsides. With his long legs on the lower slope and his short legs above, Felkin could stick to steep slopes like a tick to a dog's ear.

Felkin brought along a one-string cornstalk fiddle, Lolly-Too-Dum, which he could make sing out like a chorus of fall crickets. Younger brother was pleased no end to have Felkin live on his farm and help him.

The very next day younger brother sent Felkin to the steep field to dig holes for the seed corn. But the dirt was so hard that Felkin couldn't make a dent in it. Younger brother got a crowbar and pried the ground apart, while the horse dropped in the grains. All that day and the next the two of them worked. Still they managed to get only one row of corn planted.

The next day they started on the second row, but it was covered with rocks. No sooner did younger brother and Felkin begin planting than they smacked up against a big boulder. Wham-sock-o-diddle! Younger brother got as mad as a shovel full of hot coals.

"Why, there are more rocks on this field than dirt," he bellowed angrily. "I aim to tell my brothers right now."

He shot down the valley and hollered for the twins. His brothers came a-running. When they heard all he had to say, they pointed out that those big rocks were there on his farm to hold down all that rich dirt.

"If those rocks weren't there," Creel told him, "the crows would steal your rich dirt and sell it at the fair."

"That's the reason we closed up this end of the valley," went on Huckabuck. "We didn't want folks to sneak up there and take all that fine dirt away from you."

Younger brother felt ashamed. Oh, he knew he had no right whatsoever to complain! His older brothers were looking after him in a fit and proper fashion. He told them how sorry he was to bother them.

"Fiddle-faddle!" they exclaimed. "We forgive you."

They gave him a plow to take back. The plowshare was rusty as last year's rain. Younger brother didn't mind the rust, but he did wonder why it had no point.

"That's so it can go in any direction," Creel answered him. "It's been invented especially to use on mountain farms like yours."

One of the wooden handles had rotted away, and hornets had built a nest, which hung down under the other handle.

"That plow is so easy to use, you only need one handle," Huckabuck explained. "And a hornet's nest brings good luck to farmers, as you well know. Take it, it's yours—the best plow money can buy."

Younger brother thanked the twins again and again. Then he fetched the plow back to the mountaintop. He hitched Felkin to it at once, and they set to work. Rocks threw the plow to one side. Roots tossed it up in the air. Worms wrapped themselves around it and held it back. Felkin got madder and madder.

At last he quit. Being a horse, he was mighty unhandy with words, but he didn't have to speak out. He made it plain as the first crack of daylight that something was wrong. He sat on a stump and played his fiddle and wouldn't work another lick.

Younger brother felt miserable. He felt wretched. Here he had the best of farms with the richest of dirt. He owned a crackerjack plow and a fine horse. He worked hard. And still he couldn't make a go of farming.

He was a failure, a teetotaciously no-good farmer. The twins would be mortified when they found out that he had wasted all his dandy chances to be successful. There was nothing for him to do but leave. He wouldn't stay here any longer and shame Creel and Huckabuck. But where could he go? And what was the fastest way to get there?

He studied it out for a while and decided there was only one place for him to go. That was down. The fastest way down was to jump. It was the surest way too.

Younger brother wrote a letter to the twins thanking them for all their many kindnesses. He asked them to please come take care of his farm and his stock, since he didn't have it in mind ever to return. It was all theirs. He sent Felkin off down the valley with the letter.

Then younger brother made his way across the fields and between the boulders to where a rock stuck out from the mountain. Standing on this ledge, he looked down. There, far below, almost out of sight, was the bottom. Somewhere down there would be his new home. He turned one last time. "Good-by, farm," he sobbed out.

He shut his eyes. He took a deep breath. Holding his nose, younger brother jumped.

Chapter 2

Down plunged younger brother, whirling and spinning around like sixty. Still and all, he didn't feel any air tearing past him. He didn't hear any roaring in his ears as he rushed down toward the valley. He reckoned he wasn't falling near fast enough.

"Why, I might never reach the bottom like this," he thought. "I'll just have to help myself along."

He huffed and puffed and squirmed and kicked his feet. But something was wrong with his kicking. He could move only one leg. For a moment he was horrified. He figured he'd left a leg at the cabin, had just gone and jumped without it. And that would positively never do.

He opened one eye and peeped out. It seemed to him he was hanging upsidedown by one foot, swinging around and bumping against the rock cliff ever so often. He popped open the other eye. It was true. He wasn't falling at all. He was hanging head downward at the top of the bluff with his foot caught by a loop of vine.

" 'Tater hills and skeeter bites!" he yelled, along with a whole long string of rowdy-dowdy words. Oh, he was mad as spit! He couldn't hang there till the vine broke. He'd have to scramble back up and jump all over again.

Using cracks and holes and rock knobs, he worked himself back up to the top of the ledge. He stood up and brushed himself off. It was a good thing he had pinned his sack to his shirt. He straightened it so he could see through the holes good, then stepped back to the edge. He had to hurry up and jump and get to the bottom.

Now he wondered if he shouldn't say a little jumping verse this time, just for good luck. He knew a good one.

> "One for the preacher,
> Two for the stump,
> Three to make ready,
> And four to jump."

He practiced it a few times. He didn't want anything to go wrong this time. He kicked away the vines and roots. He cleared his throat and was ready.

Glancing down, he thought how peaceful it looked at the bottom of the valley. The creeks danced in and out among the thickets of dark hemlocks and green pines. A few cabins were scattered about with square blocks and narrow strips of fields snug around them. Here and there a rock glistened in the sunlight like some pretty on a ring. Oh, it was going to be most comforting to be down there! But then an idea struck him all of a sudden.

"Brittle as I am and falling down so tarnal far, reckon I'll hit and splinter all to pieces," he mused, half aloud.

Well, if that should happen, it'd be hard luck, but he

didn't aim to worry one whit about it now. He had two mighty fine brothers. They'd gather up every last bit of him and put him in a deep bury-hole. Over his grave they'd raise a tall headstone. Oh, he could just see that handsome stone right now, could picture it, plain as plain, inside his head! There'd be a heap of words chiseled on it. Maybe a little verse right across the top, decorated with a sprig of calico bush. Under that would be:

HERE LIES

Next would come his name, spelled out in letters as big as his hand, and . . .

Younger brother jumped straight up like he'd been stabbed with a cedar bucket. He blinked a whole gaggle of hard, fast blinks. He snorted and he squealed.

"I ain't got no name!" he wailed. "The twins got it!"

This would never do. He'd have to make sure he had a name. What if the twins had forgotten it? Then there could be no headstone. Folks would never know who was buried in his grave. He had a feeling such a thing would be enough to make him come back and haunt himself.

He turned and made his way slowly back to his cabin. His sack head was bowed with grief. It was such a heap of trouble to go on living that he wasn't sure he could manage it.

"But heck fire and tomcats," he moaned, "look how much trouble it'd be, did I happen to die from jumping."

Why, before he could die, he had to leg it down the mountainside to his brothers. He'd have to make sure they knew his name and take it from them. Then he'd have to get both him and his name back up here on the top. Finally he'd have to jump back down there in the valley, and maybe he'd be lucky enough not to splinter but land safe and sound.

"I wonder if I can make do with just one trip down there," he cried out. "Why, this way, as much traveling as I got to do up and down the mountain, I'm apt to walk myself to death long before I'm ready to jump."

He shook his head. It was certainly a knotty problem and one he didn't feel quite ready to wrestle with, not till he'd first eaten a bite or two to strengthen himself. He went to the cabin and made up a batch of ashcake to bake on the hearth. He stewed some dried peaches. He cut a thick slab off the ham hanging from a rafter.

About the time the ham was frying good, Felkin walked in. After many gestures, younger brother understood the news the horse brought. The twins were on their way up the mountain to take over the farm.

"Fine, fine, feather fine," younger brother exclaimed. "It'll save me a trip down to see them."

He lit in and told Felkin all his troubles. Felkin was a most polite and proper horse, and he listened to the bitter end without an interruption. He didn't speak out with words, but he let younger brother know he didn't believe the twins wanted to give him back his name.

"You're joshing, Felkin," younger brother told him. "If you knew how good those two have been to me, you wouldn't have such a thought. Why, they'll do anything for me. You wait. You'll see they'll be happy to give me my name. I just hope they haven't lost it or forgotten it. I'll get my name. Don't you worry."

Felkin still looked doubtful. This set younger brother to thinking. What if Felkin proved to be right? Perhaps he had best take no chances.

"If they won't, I'll make them give me my name," shouted younger brother, jumping to his feet. "But you'll have to help me. Will you, Felkin?"

The horse agreed to help, and younger brother got his hunting gun. Felkin had never in his life shot a rifle. He didn't know the first thing about frizzen pans and gun thimbles and such. Younger brother showed him how to load, how to wedge the stock to his shoulder, and how to sight down the barrel and pull the trigger.

But when Felkin found out the gun made a heap of noise

and smoke, he didn't care to hold it. He gave it back to younger brother.

"Aw, come on, Felkin. You won't have to shoot it, more than likely," younger brother told him. "They'll give me my name. I know the twins. They're generous to a fault. But just in case they won't, you jump out of your hiding place with the gun."

Then he shoved the horse out of sight under the bed. "Don't move, Felkin. Don't move a peg unless I holler for your help," he instructed.

Meanwhile, Creel and Huckabuck were making their way slowly up the mountainside. They pulled and tugged and helped each other over rocks and around slick places. The twins had always been squeezing close to each other and did everything together. They were so close that when Creel smiled, Huckabuck felt good all over. When Huckabuck had a bad case of the Short Growth, Creel took to his bed with a little bag of sow bugs tied around his neck to cure it.

Now Creel was lazy. He was so lazy that he had never in his life washed his clothes. Whenever his clothes got dirty, he just bought another pair of pants and another shirt and put them on over his old dirty ones. After years of this, he was fat with clothes. It took a heap of hard work to get him and his fat clothes up the steep mountain.

Huckabuck had skinny legs. His legs were so skinny that you had to look twice to make sure they were there at all. He was mighty ashamed of his thin shanks and lived in mortal fear that some day his breeches would suddenly fall down and everybody would see his killdeer legs and laugh at them.

Huckabuck wore a dozen pairs of galluses strapped over his shoulders and tied to the top of his pants. He had a whole store of belts wrapped around his waist, one with a big padlock. Also he had starched his breeches till they stood up by themselves, hard and straight as ironing boards. It was powerful hard to climb a mountain stiff-legged, but Huckabuck somehow managed it.

After many struggles, the twins at last reached the top

and took the path toward the cabin, side by side.

"It's sad to think we ain't got younger brother to care for," Creel said, while Huckabuck sniffled sorrowfully.

"Oh, it is," agreed Huckabuck, as Creel wiped a tear from the corner of his eye. "After all we did for him, why do you reckon younger brother wanted to run off like this?"

"I expect he wanted to help us in return for the many kind things we've done for him," Creel answered. "Poor little soul, he didn't know no way to do that except to go away and leave everything to us. He was ever a thoughty one."

"What a good brother he was," cried out Huckabuck. "They don't hardly make younger brothers like that any more these days."

Reaching the clearing, they were startled to see smoke coming out of the cabin chimney. They hid quickly behind two trees.

"Younger brother has gone away," Creel whispered. "And he left us that cabin. Who do you suppose is using it without our permission?"

"A robber with a blunderbuss," suggested Huckabuck, and he held on to the tree in fear.

"A wild band of hoop snakes maybe," said Creel, and he moved closer to his twin brother.

"A gang of salubrious twin-hating bears!"

"A pack of mad squirrels."

"A little knee-high man with screech-owl eyes."

"Escaped crawdads."

"Fierce monkey-eyed pirates."

"Stacks of Indian warriors."

The two named over every mean, scary thing there was. And they shivered and they shook.

"Let's go home and find out later," Creel said. "Folks around here in the mountains think a heap of us. They'd be mad if we went and got ourselves killed right out in daylight like this."

"True, brother." Huckabuck nodded. "We must think of others, indeed we must. It's our duty to save ourselves for the good of our friends and neighbors."

"Right-tiddly-tee-toe," Creel said, and he began to creep away.

Now younger brother had become mighty impatient waiting on his brothers. He was looking out the door when he saw them leaving. "Hold on there, you two," he called out.

"That was younger brother's voice," said Creel.

"I doubt it," Huckabuck told him. "If younger brother has gone away, I expect his voice has too."

"Hide yourself and I'll holler and see," Creel whispered. Then he cupped his mouth with his hands and shouted, "Helllloooo, the cabin. Anybody there?"

Younger brother answered, "Oh, yes, Brother Creel. All of me is right here."

The twins glanced at each other with suspicion. "How come he ain't gone?" Huckabuck wanted to know.

"Come on and sit a spell with me," younger brother called to them. "I've whopped up a scrumptious dinner-meal. It'd be neighborly of you to help me eat it."

The twins sniffed the air, and a delicious aroma of ham and baking bread came to them. Their mouths began to water.

"We'd best stay and help him with the food," Creel suggested. "Younger brother was always a finicky eater. He'll never be able to handle all the food by himself."

"Oh, indeed he won't," cried Huckabuck. "If he ate it all, he'd be sick sure. We'll just stay and help him keep well."

"It's our bound duty to protect our baby brother," Creel went on. "Stay we must."

"Get the food on the table," shouted Huckabuck. "We be a-coming."

Yet and yet, the twins were still a mite suspicious. They were cautious. They'd not risk crossing the clearing in plain sight. So off they went snicker-snack through the woods from tree to tree, and from rock to stump, keeping in the shadows.

They reached the cabin and looked under the eaves. There were only dirt-dauber nests and spider webs. They peered carefully around the corners and found nothing but weeds.

Then Creel wet his finger and held it up to check the wind. Huckabuck threw salt over his left shoulder to ward off evil. Creel wished three times on the haystack in the barnyard for good luck. Huckabuck crossed his thumbs and said, "King's X." Finally Creel lined them both up with the meridian, and they were ready.

"Do you have the sack over your head?" the twins asked. When younger brother assured them that he did, they marched inside and stopped.

"He don't look like a stranger," Creel said to Huckabuck. "He looks like our dear younger brother."

Huckabuck looked younger brother up and down. "If he jumped off this mountain, he's sure to be splintered dead, and this might be his spook come back to haunt us," he cautioned. "Best make sure."

The two went up to younger brother. Creel pinched his arm, and younger brother squealed. Huckabuck pinched his leg, and younger brother howled.

"Ooooo, that smarts terribly," younger brother wailed, dancing around on one foot, rubbing first his hurt leg, then his arm.

The twins stared at each other. "He's real flesh," exclaimed Creel. "Yes, he is," agreed Huckabuck.

"Howdy, brother," Creel said with a little bow to younger brother. "How glad we are to see you still alive."

"You're looking dandy," Huckabuck added, eying the

33

table. "And the food looks dandy too."

"It's a plumb wonder I look as well as you say," younger brother told them, "considering the fact I have to go around without a name to call my own. Everybody has a name but me. Felkin's got one. His fiddle's got one, and the tunes he plays on it got the prettiest kinds of names. You two have both got names."

The twins nodded. "And you got my name, ain't you?" asked younger brother. "You ain't forgot it? Or lost it or anything?"

"We got it, safe and sound," Creel said. "Rest easy that we ain't forgot it," Huckabuck told him. "We ain't the forgetting kind."

"Well, I'm mighty much obliged to you for keeping it for me," younger brother said. "But now I'm wanting it in the worst kind of way. Tell me my name and then we'll eat." He leaned forward so as not to miss a single syllable.

"Pee-shaw and posh, younger brother, you can have my name," Creel offered generously. "I'll take it back when you're dead and through with it." He pulled up a bench and sat at the table. Breaking off half of the ashcake, he spread butter over it.

"No, I ain't going to take it," younger brother told him. "It wouldn't be *my* name."

"Then take my name and welcome," Huckabuck insisted. He stood by the table and commenced cramming ham into his mouth.

"No, you must tell me what my very own name is," younger brother begged. "Please."

"Pour a little of that gravy over my bread, younger brother," Creel ordered. "What a treat you be giving your poor brothers! We don't eat this fine at our house."

"More ham for me, brother, and some of those stewed peaches," commanded Huckabuck. "You're the best cook in creation, younger brother."

All the while younger brother waited on the twins, he pleaded with them to tell him his name. The twins paid no attention but ate steadily till there wasn't a smidgen of food left and all the pots and skillets were licked clean.

At last younger brother saw that he was getting nowhere this way. Felkin had been right. They didn't want to give him his name. It was a terrible thing. But it must be they didn't realize how much he wanted it. He would have to show them.

"Now you listen here," he cried and tried to look as fierce as a sack of bobcats. "I aim to get my name. Come out, Felkin."

The horse slid out from under the bed and stood there with the gun. "Hold on a moment, Felkin," said younger brother. "I'll fix it where one bullet will get them both."

He moved Huckabuck over beside Creel and made Creel sit up a little straighter. Then younger brother got behind Felkin and helped him aim the rifle. "Move back just a hair, Huckabuck."

Huckabuck did as he was told. "That's just right, and don't move, brothers," younger brother commanded. Standing before them, he said, "Quick now, my name, or Felkin'll shoot you dead."

"What! You'd kill us and waste all that good food you made us eat?" Creel protested.

"It's sinful to waste food, younger brother," Huckabuck scolded him. "And besides, you ain't doing this right a-tall."

"What am I doing wrong?" younger brother wanted to know.

"Why, everybody and their kin know you have to first say to folks you're killing: 'Give me your money or your lives,'" Creel said.

"That's right," went on Huckabuck, "and when we don't hand over our money, then it's fair and square to shoot us."

Felkin snorted and tossed his mane and tried every which way to get younger brother to pay no attention to such foolishness. But younger brother had always listened to his brothers and minded what they told him.

"All right, I'll do as you say," he agreed. He drew himself up and crossed his arms on his chest and in his sternest voice said, "Give me your money or give me your lives."

Creel began, "Take our lives, for we're . . ."

". . . saving our money for our old age," finished Huckabuck.

The twins laughed and laughed. Felkin groaned and

ground his teeth together. Younger brother was hurt in his feelings. He had done as they asked, and then they had tricked him. It wasn't fair. So he hollered out, "My name or Felkin shoots!"

The twins turned and looked at Felkin and the rifle. Then they busted out laughing again. They laughed till tears poured from their eyes.

"I don't see nothing so all-fired funny," said younger brother. "Shoot, Felkin, and shoot to kill."

Felkin pulled the trigger.

Chapter 3

The gun roared. There was a blinding flash. Smoke billowed from the rifle and filled the cabin room. "Oh, my good gravy!" cried younger brother. "I shouldn't ought to have let Felkin kill the twins. And they made the worst kind of smoke too." He fell to choking and coughing.

But when the room cleared, there sat the twins, still whooping and laughing. It exasperated younger brother terribly.

"Dern your hide, Felkin. You missed them," raved younger brother. "Now, Creel, don't you and Huckabuck move a hair till I can get the rifle loaded again."

He reached for the powder horn on the mantelpiece. Something came humming and buzzing toward him, and younger brother ducked. "There's that big ole skeeter come to steal some more butter so him and his young 'uns can rub it on their feet and go sliding down the mountainside," he said. "Dern, it's a pesky varmint."

It went tearing around the room again, but slower than before. On the third time around, it was just barely going, and Creel reached out and grabbed it. Then he handed it to younger brother.

It was the round lead bullet that Felkin had just shot. Younger brother was taken aback and mad too. "A body can't depend on nothing going right these days," he yelled. He shook his fist at the lead ball. "How come you didn't do what you was supposed to do?" he wanted to know.

The bullet didn't bother to answer, but Creel did for it. "That bullet went perzackly right," he said. He turned and pointed at the gun Felkin held. "Look at that barrel."

Younger brother felt mighty foolish when he looked. He'd forgotten he'd bent his rifle barrel in a curve so it would shoot around the rocks and hit something on the other side. It was the onliest kind of gun he could use on his mountain farm.

Felkin hung his head and looked ashamed. He should have noticed that. The twins said it had been a fine dinner, but now it was time to leave.

Younger brother threw himself between them and the doorway. He'd fight them both to keep them here. What did he have handy to hit them with? An almanac, a bacon rind, a turnip with no sides, the clapper from a cowbell, Felkin—oh, oh, there wasn't a thing for him to use! What could he do? Suddenly he knew.

"Whoa there, brothers," he said, holding up his hand. "Now you know I am ugly."

"Yes, younger brother, you are." Creel nodded. "You're so ugly that if you didn't wear that sack over your head, sleep couldn't slip up on you at night."

"You're so ugly," Huckabuck told him, "that one single look and you could knock over a catamount, bring down a flock of fat turkeys from the treetops, deaden an acre of white oaks, and frighten a band of snakes up out of their dens."

"Take our word for it, younger brother. You've got the worst case of uglies in all of Tennessee," Creel spoke. "But we don't mind."

"No, sir, billy goat, we don't mind," Huckabuck said. "We still love you, for you're our wonderful brother."

"Then if I'm as ugly as you say, it might just be too bad for you was I to take my sack off," younger brother said. "And if you don't tell me my name right here and now, I'll jerk this onion sack off." He took hold of one edge and began to raise it.

The twins clutched each other and held on tight, white and trembling. Their eyes rolled with fear. The breath rattled in and out of their throats. At last they calmed themselves, and Creel turned to younger brother.

"All right, we were going to tell you anyway, only we're not ready yet," Creel explained. "We haven't got all the rules made up."

"Rules? What rules?" asked younger brother.

"Why, the rules," said Huckabuck. "There's rules for everything. There's rules for planting corn and 'taters; there's rules for feeding chickens; there's rules for adding two and two, and making soup and standing on your head. Did you ever hear tell of rain falling up? No, you ain't, for it follows the rules and falls down."

"Did you ever hear tell of blue leaves on a tree?" asked Creel. "Not in this world. The rules say green leaves, and green leaves is what you get. Ain't that right?"

Younger brother scratched his chest. Of course he knew about rules. Anybody could see things went by rules. If he'd only thought a little harder, he'd have known that names had to go by rules too.

"Now the rules say," went on Huckabuck, "that before we can give you back your name, you must raise bigger 'taters and bigger corn than we raise."

"Course now, you're a heap better farmer than us, and you got a better farm, so you'll be sure to win," Creel explained. "But that's the way the rules go."

The twins told all about out of bounds, double gammons, and the rules for melding and passing whammies to the other side. They all seemed like good rules to younger brother, though mostly he couldn't understand them. And when it was agreed to, the twins rushed away home.

Summer was on them, lazy warm days when it would have been proper to sleep in the shade or soak in the cold spring. But every day younger brother and Felkin watered their fields. They chopped down the weeds. They shooed crows away from the corn and rabbits out of the potato fields. Both of them worked everlasting hard from first dawning till candlelight.

The corn grew straight and tall. Each day during the summer it rose up, higher and higher. It grew so high that it took both Felkin and younger brother to see to the top of it. Felkin looked till his eyes got tired, then younger brother took up where Felkin left off, and he looked and looked till he saw the very tip top.

"That's mighty pretty corn, Felkin," younger brother commented one day, standing at the field's edge and admiring it. "But we got to chop about half of it down."

It didn't hardly seem right to Felkin to work so hard growing it and then whack it down.

"Look back there among those stalks," said younger brother.

Down underneath the corn, it was dark. Lightning bugs glimmered and glowed there, and hooty owls flew about hunting just like it was nighttime.

"Can't you see the corn's so tall, it's blocking off the sunlight," younger brother said. "Ain't you been noticing how the sun's quit coming over our mountain. Our corn's grown so tall, the sun can't get over it but has to detour around the corn."

Felkin nodded. It was awful dark on the mountaintop for high noon of an August day. Younger brother had lit a lantern to help them see the way.

"And the 'taters ain't getting enough sunlight with the sun going some other way," younger brother pointed out.

On the side of the mountain, the potato plants had begun to wither and shrivel. The patch on top looked poorly too.

"Go get the crosscut saw, and we'll start cutting down the corn," younger brother said.

But Felkin wouldn't agree to it. He worked out a plan to save the 'taters and leave the corn standing too. They went to the edge of the mountain with a heap of croker-sacks. Now here at this particular spot, there was a fierce echo. No matter how softly a body might whisper, the echo would fling it back loud and strong.

Younger brother stood there and said, "Sunshine." And

when "Sunshine" came booming back, he and Felkin caught it in one of the sacks. They toted the sunshine to the potato fields and spread it all around nice and even. The plants perked up at once.

At the end of the day, the 'taters were saved. "It just goes to show a fellow needs a good horse around to help him farm," younger brother told Felkin. Felkin agreed with that. He got out his fiddle and played a tune to ease the weariness from his body. Fiddle music is as good as herb tonic at such times, and Felkin knew this. He played till the first whippoorwill called and then went to bed. Younger brother had been asleep long since.

The moon rose bright as a silver penny. By its light, two figures crept up the mountainside. They had shovels and axes and all manner of tools. When they reached the edge of younger brother's potato patch, they stopped to rest.

"Listen," whispered Creel. "You hear that talking?"

"Hide quick," Huckabuck said. "Somebody's seen us."

"No, it's coming from underneath our feet," Creel told him. He got down on his knees and put his ear to the ground.

"Get over. Move over. Give me more room," said a gravelly voice.

There were a bunch of groans and a heap of grunting.

"Lay over, lay over. You're squeezing me," a deep voice spoke.

The field rumbled and shook like it'd been hit by an earthquake.

"It's those 'taters," said Creel, getting to his feet. "They ain't got enough room. There's so many of them underground and they're so big, they're crowding each other out of the rows."

"Well, that means younger brother is growing better potatoes than us," Huckabuck said. "I'm proud of him. But he's in trouble because he ain't treating his 'taters fair and square."

"Oh, Brother Huckabuck, you're right, just right as rainfall." Creel nodded. "The courts can be powerful hard on a fellow for torturing 'taters."

"The High Sheriff'll slap him in jail afore he can say naked rabbit," Huckabuck continued. "I don't want our sweet younger brother in the workhouse for ninety-nine years and a day. We'd best save him quick."

They set to work, and with their axes they chopped off the end of each of the potato rows. The potatoes came rolling out and went off down the mountainside like loud thunder.

When every row was empty, Creel smiled. "Helping

'taters and helping folks gives me the best feeling in the world."

"True, brother, so true," Huckabuck agreed. "I'm tired but mighty happy. Younger brother won't go to jail for tormenting helpless critters, and the 'taters got plenty of room to grow down there in the valley near us."

With arms around each other, they made their way back to their cabin, leaving their tools hidden in the bushes in case younger brother needed their help again.

The next morning Felkin was up early to inspect the crops. The corn was tall and straight and as pretty as any Felkin had ever seen. It was still growing, but some stalks had grown so fast that the roots had been pulled up out of the ground. Felkin shook his head. It would be a day's hard work to tie rocks to the corn roots to hold them in the ground.

He moved on to the potato patch on the side of the mountain. Something had happened to it! The rows were empty. There was not a potato in the whole field. Thieves! Felkin knew it! Somebody had been there and left footprints everywhere.

He fetched younger brother, and younger brother was powerful put out when he saw what had happened. "Now who could have stole my potaters?" he asked. "I reckon it was some new kind of 'tater bug, for I've never seen a regular 'tater bug leave such footprints as these. And look here, they've left their axes in the bushes. I never knew a 'tater bug to use axes before."

Felkin wanted to take the axes away, but younger brother said no, he'd never stolen anything in his life, not even an ax that belonged to a potato bug. He headed for the cabin.

Felkin looked and looked, but he couldn't find a single potato left in the field. He began to cry a little. But just then younger brother came running back. "Oh, I'm going to get my name now," he whooped. "Come and see the monstrous big one in the field on top!"

Younger brother led the way, laughing and shouting. There sticking up in the middle of the field was a knob of earth, as tall and smooth as an Indian mound. It hadn't been there the day before when the two of them were spreading the sunlight around.

Younger brother showed Felkin the hole where he'd dug
into the ground. The horse came up and looked in the opening. There was something hard and solid there, and he in-
spected it mighty close and careful. After a sniff and a nibble
or two, Felkin agreed this was indeed a giant potato.

"Yiiiiipppppee!" shouted younger brother. "I've won, I've
won. Why, this 'tater's big enough to feed a regiment of
hungry Tennessee soldiers a whole winter season."

Felkin agreed.

49

"Now we can't dig all of it up out of the ground," younger brother exclaimed. "But we can clear the dirt away so it can be seen by one and all."

They set to work, and all day long they shoveled the dirt off the potato. Every once in a while, younger brother would stand back a ways to admire the potato. "Hi there, ole 'tater!" he'd call out with a cheerful grin and a wave of the hand. Then he would run around to the far side and wave and holler out again, "Hi there, ole 'tater on this side."

Oh, it was good to have a big ole potato to call out to! And it would be good to have a name too. He could hardly wait to find out what it was. Then he went back to work, humming happily.

They finished up in the late afternoon as shadows began to stretch across the field. What a sight lay there in the twilight—a potato, big as all outdoors, with brown skin like tree bark and a million eyes!

"I feel powerful set up," said younger brother. "I've won my name, and I did it following the rules, fair and square. Just think, Felkin. Tomorrow I'll have a name."

He broke into a jig, whirling and capering around and around the potato. Felkin got his fiddle and played while younger brother kicked up his heels and frolicked. As he danced, he sang:

"What, oh what will my pretty name be?
Hilo, Jick Jack, or Red Stavin Lee,
Laidley or Sassafras or Big Tuckerhoe,
Smathers or Higgley or Gourd-head Mo?
Sing whiddle compolly whodangle complay.

"Long or short, it'll suit me to a tee.
It'll be mine, all mine, and I'll be me,
Me, all me, squantolating about,
With a sassy new name for folks to shout.
Sing whiddle compolly whodangle complay.

"What'll my name be, what'll folks call,
When I gallop by on my fierce catawaul?
Hank O'Leay, Shammin, or Nolichucky Jack?
Whatsoever it be, I'm sure to answer back.
Sing whiddle compolly whodangle complay."

When he had finished, younger brother said, "I'll fetch the twins up here first thing tomorrow morning. They'll tell me my name. Then we'll have a scrumptious jollifying party to celebrate."

51

Chapter 4

The twins didn't wait for the party younger brother planned the next day. They arrived that night. As they slipped creepy-crawly across younger brother's potato field, something huge and black and bumpy suddenly rose up before them.

"It's a monster!" screamed Creel, and his ribs all jangled together with fright.

"Oh, help!" shrieked Huckabuck, and he leaped to Creel's shoulders for protection.

But Creel had already jumped for Huckabuck's shoulders. Scared most nigh to death, they kept hopping up on each other's shoulders, rising higher and higher into the sky, twin on top of twin. Up and up and up they climbed, and they might have been climbing to this very day if Huckabuck hadn't missed.

He jumped a mite too hard and shot past Creel's shoulders. Though he twisted and turned and tried every way to scramble back, he didn't make it. Down he fell, whirling around and around. He hit the ground with a terrible jolt. Here came Creel right behind him. He landed with all his fat clothes smack on top of Huckabuck and mashed him flat.

Creel wasn't hurt, but he could see that horrible monster waiting right there to pounce on him. He had to hide quick, but there was no place to get except under Huckabuck. He jumped to his feet and tried to lift Huckabuck. He couldn't. Huckabuck was mashed so flat that Creel couldn't so much as get his fingers under him.

"Oh, you are a coward!" screamed Creel. "For you have pigged the only hiding place and won't let me have none of it!"

And he sank to his knees and begged Huckabuck to let him have just a crack. Huckabuck never so much as mumbled.

Now Creel was scared worse than ever. He could see that old thing rise up. He made sure it was coming closer; he made certain it was reaching for him with big old skinny arms. His knees cracked, his toes and ears turned green and curled up, and three pairs of his pants turned to ice.

Finally Creel saw that the thing wasn't moving. It hadn't come any closer. He picked up his courage and looked at it straight. "I believe to my soul it's a 'tater," he told Huckabuck. "I don't believe it's a man-eating 'tater, so we're safe, thank goodness."

He took out his knife and slipped the blade under Huckabuck and worked him loose from the ground. He scraped off the flatness and beat a little wind back into him. Then Huckabuck was as good as ever.

The two went over to look at the potato. They kicked it with their square-toed shoes. They punched it and jabbed it with sticks. Nothing happened. They got a ladder from the barn and bravely climbed up on top of the potato. They walked around, inspecting it, and scared up a flock of turkeys roosting there for the night.

"I'm satisfied this is a huge 'tater, through and through," Creel said. He shook his head sadly. "And I'm terribly sorry for younger brother. He's gone and raised a potato too big to get on a wagon."

"Well, it won't go in a skillet, that's for sure," Huckabuck put in. "So our poor brother can't fry it."

"I doubt he can bake it either," Creel pointed out. "It'd take all the wood on these mountains, and he'd likely have to bring in a forest or two from Caroliny to bake it good and crisp."

"I believe it would just about fit in the river," Huckabuck declared. "That 'tater would make a fine dam, but it might poison the water and kill all the fish."

"Whatever in the world is our desperate younger brother going to do?" asked Creel. "He's got himself into a terrible combumptious situation. We must think of some way to help him."

"Oh, you are right, Brother Creel." Huckabuck smiled. "Howsomever, helping younger brother to get rid of this troublesome 'tater will take all night. Do you think we should give up our sleep to do it?"

"Yes! Yes! We must! We must! This is no time for us to think of ourselves," cried Creel.

"Right again," said Huckabuck. "We must not show the white flag. We must bite the bullet; we must stand tall in the saddle; we must help!"

"Brothers must always help each other!" exclaimed Creel.

"Would I be showing a true helping spirit if right about here, on this end, I chopped a friendly opening in the potato?" asked Huckabuck.

"Oh, you would, brother, you would indeedy." Creel nodded. "And to do my part, I'll drive up the cows and pigs and chickens, for all of us here on the farm, folks as well as animals, must pitch in together and help out."

Creel rushed off toward the barn. Huckabuck picked up his ax and began to chop away at the tough potato skin. Chips flew in a steady stream and, every once in a while, a shower of sparks when a hard, knotty place was struck. But Huckabuck never let up. He flailed away for all he was worth. The ax blade glowed red-hot. The opening got bigger and bigger. At last Huckabuck cut through the skin. The inside was soft and white. He sliced away great chunks of it with no trouble at all.

Huckabuck quit when the animals came crowding up and began to eat at the insides of the potato. There was all manner of juicy smackings and happy grunts and squeals and contented clucks. Never had younger brother's animals had such a feast. They ate and ate right on up inside the 'tater, out of sight.

The twins left then and headed for the cornfield.

"You know, brother," Creel said with a sob, "life is fickle and chancy at best. It seems to me most anything can happen."

"It generally does." Huckabuck nodded. "Whatever do you reckon could happen to this field of tall corn?"

"You know, I expect that younger brother has forgotten that good farmers always rotate their crops," Creel mused.

"It looks like an easily turned field," Huckabuck said. He looked around at Creel, and Creel turned and looked at him. They nodded to each other.

While katydids hollered and the moon rolled across one side of the sky and the big bear swung around on the other side, the twins worked quietly but steadily. Just before sunup, they finished and started off for home.

They were not more than a stone's throw down the mountainside when younger brother bounced out of bed. He was too excited to stay under the covers any longer but had to go outside to admire his giant potato.

One look and he felt sure he was still in bed and dreaming a bad dream. He rubbed his eyes. He poked a finger into each ear and rattled it good and hard. Taking a deep breath, he looked again. It was true, as real as daylight. His potato was gone. There was nothing left of it but a wrinkled, warty, scrambled mess.

He walked over and picked up one edge of the skin. Two chickens waddled out. A pig, so fat it couldn't walk, rolled from under the flap of skin off toward the barn. Then out came cows, more pigs and chickens, possums, coons, wood rats, crickets, moles, a deer or two, snails, slugs, jay birds, toads, shitepokes, fly-by-nights, blue peters, hang-on-the-limbs, thumpers, butterballs, sixteen field streaks, and an alligator looking for a drink of water.

Younger brother dropped the skin and sniffed. "It's gone into the everlasting hereafter." He reached up under the sack and wiped the tears from his eys. "It was such a nice friendly 'tater, I'll miss it terribly."

It was gone, and the chance to get his name with it was gone too. He'd never grow another potato that size. There was nothing but grief in this world, he felt. Oh, if there was just some way to commit suicide without killing himself, he would, right this very minute! Life was a heap of trouble for him most days and hardly worth it the rest of the time.

Felkin came hobbling up. He said nothing, but he poked around the remains, studying the ground. He pointed out to younger brother all the footprints, the chips of potato skin, and the ax.

"It's hard for me to believe the twins would do me any meanness," younger brother answered, "though that ax has 'Creel & Huckabuck' carved on the handle. Likely some bad person has stolen it and come up here, jealous of my 'tater. Brothers don't do mean things to their other brothers, Felkin. You got to understand that. We're blood kin and love each other."

Younger brother turned away. "I won't cry over a lost 'tater. I still have my tall, tall . . ." He stopped. A terrible moan came up from deep inside him. Where was his field of corn? Where the corn had been last night, when he went to bed, there was now nothing but an empty field with a hole in the middle.

It didn't take the two of them long to find out what had happened. During the night the field had been turned completely over. The corn was now underground. And in rotating the field, an old coal mine had been turned up. The entrance was still propped open with stout wooden beams. An old hermit who made his home in the mine was sitting in the entrance.

Felkin and younger brother rushed up to him and wanted to know who had done this terrible thing. Now it had been so long since the hermit had spoken to anyone that he had most nigh forgot how. His speaking apparatus was all clogged up with rust and dust and bats and things. Felkin and younger brother took him by his heels and turned him upside down and shook him till all his tubes and cords were cleared out.

After that, the hermit had to remember the right words. At first he remembered the wrong ones. He remembered "bandicoot" and "Morris chair" and "astrological chart" and "electoral college." Felkin and younger brother danced while they waited for him to remember. Gracious, how they danced! Swing your partner, dosey-do! Ladies to the right and gents to the left. Birdie in the cage and round you go!

Finally the hermit remembered the proper words. "It was Creel and Huckabuck done it, out of sheer ornery meanness," he said. "They don't want you to leave here. They don't want you to have a name. They're shamed of you, for they don't hanker for folks to know they got a ugly young brother."

Younger brother was put out mightily. Oh, he was peeved! He was angry and furious and wrathful. He was mad! Finally Felkin had to take him to the smokehouse and put him in the curing trough and salt him down like meat, to keep him from spoiling. To soothe him, Felkin took his fiddle and played the ballad about the poison eels and the one about the sow taking the measles and a whole bunch of gay devil ditties.

At last younger brother was calm. He announced that he was going out into the world and find himself a name and live like decent folks. "Bring your fiddle, Felkin, and come with me."

But Felkin wouldn't come. He figured with two of his legs longer on one side than on the other, it was better for him to stay on the mountain. Folks would likely stare at him in the lowlands and laugh at how ridiculous he looked.

"Bosh, Felkin. I doubt folks will notice your legs nor this sack on my head either," younger brother said. "I don't know. I've never been off this here mountain. But I wouldn't be surprised if everybody didn't have something wrong with them. The twins're scared to death of their shadows and strange noises. Creel won't wash. Huckabuck worries about his breeches falling down. Likely everybody everywhere has peculiarities. Come on."

Still, Felkin hemmed and hawed and held back. He pointed out there was no way to leave the mountain. The twins had blocked the onliest way.

"The old hermit'll let us go through his mine," younger brother said. "Wherever it comes out, it's bound to be a better place than here."

The horse agreed then. Younger brother led the way. Felkin followed, clutching his fiddle. Down, down through the dark mine they went. The walls were wet and slimy, the floor littered with fallen rocks. They turned and twisted this way and that till both were giddy and mixed-up. When at last they came out, they were way over in a county in North Carolina, a whole week earlier by the calendar, with the sun shining from the wrong part of the sky.

Younger brother refused to worry about such things. "Felkin, I'm rid of the twins forever and that's what counts!" he cried. "Oh, smell this lovely pure-dee outside fresh air!"

Then they started off. Younger brother was sure the road led to some town. He had never been to a settlement and was terribly anxious to find one. Oh, what sights he hoped to see! What fine times he hoped to have talking to all the folks there! However, it was impossible to hurry on account of Felkin. He limped along slow as jelly on his uneven legs, but younger brother would never dream of leaving him behind. They pushed along the road as best they could. Still, by nightfall, they hadn't reached a town. They slept in a haystack, tired and mighty hungry.

"I could do with a piece of that ham I left hanging on the cabin rafter and some corn-meal mush and . . ." muttered younger brother. But Felkin was snoring fit to bust. Younger brother wedged a pillow of hay under his head and went to sleep too.

Now all this time, though younger brother didn't know it, Creel and Huckabuck were coming closer and closer. They had long since discovered that younger brother had escaped from the mountaintop. And now they were running to catch him and fetch him back.

"For," said Creel, "he is a danger to innocent folks running around loose, he is so ugly."

"He's an epidemic of ugliness and ought to be returned to his fine farm," Huckabuck said. "He'll be happy there."

So they hurried through the night. And next morning before younger brother had rubbed the hay out of his eyes, they were standing in the road waiting for him. The twins looked at younger brother and Felkin. Younger brother looked back. He was a little scared.

"Well, howdy," he cried out. "I'm proud to see you. You can come journeying along with us, if you like."

The twins just went on looking.

"But I ain't going back with you," he went on. And then he thought that might not be true, for everywhere he turned, there was a twin and none of them looked friendly. Unless he learned to run straight up in the air, they had him caught, good and proper.

Chapter 5

"Dear, dear younger brother." Creel smiled. "Oh, how glad we are to find you safe and sound!" His smile grew bigger. His mouth stretched wider and wider. It opened so wide that younger brother saw past Creel's pointed teeth all the way down to his dirty toenails.

It was a horrible sight and scared younger brother so that the sack spun around on his head. He looked the other way, and there was Huckabuck. And Huckabuck wasn't any easier to look at. He clapped his hands over the eyeholes of his sack. He didn't want to see either one of the twins.

"How worried we've been," Huckabuck cried. "How grieved to think that our younger brother was wandering about the world, lost and hungry, and we weren't there to help him."

"We've come to take you back, dear helpless brother."

"We miss you, sweet younger brother."

"Our lives are empty and useless without you."

Now younger brother knew the twins didn't mean what they said. It had taken him a long time to learn this lesson, but now he'd learned it good. He wasn't going to listen to them or believe them. He wasn't going to be scared of them. He was just going to walk away from them.

But his legs didn't seem to know this. His knees were weak and rattly, and his feet were terrible heavy and slow. No matter how hard he tried, he couldn't run or walk or even creep away from them.

"Felkin," younger brother whispered, "do you know any way to make feet go? I've tried 'Giddy-up' and 'Git' and 'Hi ho, feet, go it!' None of 'em work."

Felkin seemed to ponder for a minute or so. The twins shuffled closer and closer and closer. Younger brother strained and twisted to lift his feet, but he just couldn't.

"Now come along, younger brother," said Creel and reached to grab him.

"Felkin! Quick!" yelled younger brother.

"And now we . . ."

". . . got you, younger brother."

At the very moment the twins jumped for younger brother, Felkin leaned over and bit him in the leg. Younger brother screamed with pain and took off running. The twins snatched and got nothing, and their heads cracked against one another loud as a thunderclap.

"Come on, Felkin," called younger brother from the woods.

He was wasting his breath, for the horse had lit out running right behind younger brother, but Felkin just wasn't able to keep up. Try as he might, the very best he could do on his uneven legs was to rock and wobble along, going six different directions at once, yet getting nowhere. He could fall to the ground and get farther ahead than he could standing up and running. His joints grated and cracked. Bones stuck out at queer spots, and his ears changed places every time his feet hit the ground.

Finally Felkin sank down, worn out and most nigh jarred out of shape. He waved to younger brother to go on without him.

"Felkin, you're the onliest friend I got, and I won't leave you here for the twins," younger brother cried. "Goodness knows what they'd do to you now."

What could he do to save them? He'd hardly ever done any thinking, and it might be it was too late to start. "Now don't you worry," he told Felkin. "We'll stick together and get out of this somehow or other. I'm bound to think of something." And he had to do it mighty quick. He could hear the twins a-thrashing through the woods toward them.

"Help! Help!" younger brother shouted. "Oh, help!" It was all he knew to do when times were parlous and things were desperate.

The crashing and rattling came near. Younger brother clutched Felkin, and the horse clutched his fiddle. All three were scared to death. But it wasn't the twins who came tearing from between the trees and across the clearing toward them. It was a man pushing an empty wheelbarrow.

Younger brother jumped up, waving his hands. "Hold on, hold on there, please, Mister feller."

The man stopped. Younger brother explained that he

would like to borrow the wheelbarrow to let the horse ride in. "We're running from a bunch of twins, and Felkin here has done give out. We got to get away, and we can with your wheelbarrow. Please, we won't use it long."

"I can't do it, confound you," the man panted. "See that flock of ducks flying up yonder? See how close together they're keeping? Well, last year I shot into that flock and killed a dozen or so. But they're packed so tight together, the dead ones won't fall out. They just keep flying along with the live ducks. But I killed them, and they're my ducks. Some day they'll come dropping down. When they do, I aim to catch them in this here wheelbarrow. I don't want 'em to fall to the ground and get bruised. It ruins the meat. Duck is mighty fine eating, and I sure aim to enjoy these."

"Felkin can sit in the wheelbarrow and catch the ducks as they fall," younger brother suggested. "And until they fall, he can play some music while me and you push him along."

"All right," agreed the man. "I'll let you and Felkin use my wheelbarrow. But if I do, you'll have to keep that fiddle quiet. I can't abide the scritching-scratching of cornstalk fiddles. But I declare, I do like riddles. Ain't no riddle ever been born I can't answer."

"Is that how you make your living?" asked younger brother. "You must be powerful clever to earn your way like that."

"Shucks, now, I just do it for fun," the man answered. "Everybody knows that, and everybody knows me. I'm Pig Eye. I'm called that 'cause I can spit in a pig's eye at twenty feet."

"Goodness, you're full of surprises," gasped younger brother. "That's the finest kind of spitting."

"I like riddles better than spitting. Come on. Them ducks is about to get clear away." Pig Eye pointed to the flock going off over the treetops. "You can ask me riddles as we follow 'em."

Felkin sat in the wheelbarrow. Pig Eye grabbed the handles and began to push. He gathered speed quickly and was soon running right underneath the flock of ducks.

"Ask me a riddle."

"All right, Mister Pig Eye," said younger brother. He cogitated a bit and then asked, "What has two heads, one tail, four legs on one side and two legs on the other?"

"I bet it's a whop-sided nutmeg," answered Pig Eye.

Younger brother shook his head. Pig Eye cried, "Now don't tell me the answer. Let me guess. I'll get it sooner or later. I know a heap of answers. I save 'em in a little book. I got books and books of answers."

They whipped in and out among the trees. Every once in a while, there was a loud squawking from the ducks overhead. Pig Eye guessed again. "Is it a dried-up sulphur spring?" Younger brother shook his head. "Is it an egg? A needle and thread? A smoking chimney and a scolding wife? Them's some of the best answers I got for riddles."

Younger brother tore along beside Pig Eye, shaking his head. He'd never run so much or so fast in his life. Felkin was holding on for dear life, for every once in a while they'd hit a rock and almost lose him.

They went down a road and then cut across a meadow. Younger brother glanced back. And oh, forevermore, the twins were chasing them in a wind wagon! There was a big white sail, and behind it sat Creel squeezing a pair of bellows and blowing air against the sail. How it billowed out! How the four wheels turned and whirled them along!

"Faster!" yelled younger brother.

"That's not the answer, is it?" asked Pig Eye. Younger brother shook his head. "Good, for you mustn't tell me. I'll get it. Now let me see. Is is three rows of succotash and a short-handled judge?"

"Faster! They're gaining!" younger brother screamed. As he looked back again, he saw Huckabuck stand up and throw a handful of rocks at them. Younger brother laughed. Huckabuck couldn't hit a well sitting inside it in the bucket. They were safe.

Now just that very minute an awful thing happened. Pig Eye's flock of ducks got excited at all the goings on, and they spread out just the least little bit. But it was enough. One duck fell from the flock, and then another and another and two and three and eight, and here, there, and every which way yonder.

Pig Eye ran hither and thither trying to catch them in the wheelbarrow, but instead, the barrow turned over and Felkin and Pig Eye went rolling in among the birds. Ducks were thumping down all over the woods.

"Run for your lives," cried younger brother. "We'll all be drowned."

But everywhere they turned, there were ducks and more ducks and getting deeper all the while. Younger brother knew that, for once in his life, he must do something and do it quick. At once he found two flat sticks eddying about on top of the ducks. He picked up the wheelbarrow and threw

Felkin and Pig Eye in it. Then he jumped on too. Using the pieces of wood for paddles, he soon rowed them out into the open, away from the ducks.

Then behind him he heard voices crying, "Help! Help!" He looked back, and there were Creel and Huckabuck, going down for the fifth time and screaming like pitiful buzz saws.

Younger brother knew there was no help for it. He ran back to the edge of the pool of ducks and offered a hand to each of the twins. They grabbed hold, and he pulled them to safety. As soon as they saw they were saved, they leered and winked at each other. They held on tight to younger brother's hands.

"Now come along with us, dear good brother," they cried, "back to your bee-yutiful mountain farm."

Younger brother tried to get loose. He struggled and hollered and kicked and fussed, but those twins hung on like glue, like leeches, like sticking plaster, and like a mud turtle hangs on to somebody's big toe if he ever gets a hold of it.

The twins started to drag younger brother down the road. But Pig Eye ran up and stopped them. "Wait, wait," he hollered, "for I have got to know the answer to this riddle. Younger brother, what has two heads, one tail, four legs on one side and two legs on the other? Tell me."

"I ain't got the least idea," younger brother replied. "You said ask you a riddle. I figured you'd know the answer."

When Pig Eye heard this, he was fit to be tied. He ran

72

off cussing and yelling, and if you ever meet anybody who's a good spitter and asks you the answer to that riddle, it's likely Pig Eye.

Now the twins began to pull younger brother down the road, and he had no choice but to go, for they had him fairly. Felkin followed along behind. He still had his fiddle. It was all full of feathers, and all the tunes he tried to play came out all fluffy and covered with down, and some of them even quacked, but he kept trying.

Now night began to fall, and the shadows grew long. It was a dark and lonely road they were traveling. Noisy bushes lined the way. Things flitted by and loomed large and dwindled down and sometimes hollered and often moaned. Younger brother wasn't scared, for things often did this on his mountain farm. He knew it was just the nighttime's way of settling in.

But the twins were scared, for all their lives they had been so busy being mean, they hadn't had time to notice such things, and now it frightened them terribly. They shivered and shook and kept trying to look on all sides at once.

Then in the road up ahead, they saw something big and black. Creel called a halt. He pointed ahead. "Oh, it's something fierce waiting for us!" he cried and shuddered.

"We'd best not move till it leaves," whispered Huckabuck. "Give it a chance to get away. Don't rouse it up, anybody."

Felkin sat down, for he was glad of a chance to rest. The brothers stood still. "I hear it growling," said Creel. "And I see it move in and out as it breathes," whispered Huckabuck.

"I don't want to be eaten on such a pretty night," moaned Creel.

"I was saving myself for some other time," Huckabuck wailed. "What can we do?"

Creel stood on one foot so there wouldn't be too much of him handy to be eaten if something hungry popped out at them. Huckabuck filled his pockets with air in case he was too scared later to breathe. Then Creel put his hands over Huckabuck's eyes, and Huckabuck placed his over Creel's ears.

In order to do this, they had to let go of younger brother. Now younger brother had good eyes. He could tell that thing in the road was nothing but a big black leather chest that somebody had lost. He didn't tell the others, though.

Instead, he turned to the twins where they were trying to wrap themselves around each other like a pair of snakes, and he said, "Oh, brothers, you have been so good to me for so many years. Now I want to repay you. I will go attack this fierce old thing. It may be it will eat me up, but if it does, it will be too slow and sleepy to eat you or even chase you. So when I'm gone, you run along home as fast as ever you can, and remember me kindly."

The twins were too busy trembling to say anything. Felkin would have bade younger brother good-by, but he was too busy pulling the feathers off his fiddle.

Younger brother tiptoed slowly down the road toward the chest. When he came near, there was a terrible fierce howl. Younger brother never flinched. He began to circle about the chest, inching closer and closer. At last he jumped forward and flung open the lid. He put his hands over his eyes and screamed and screamed. But he managed to slam down the top and flung himself across the chest and held it tight. Now the thing really roared. Younger brother hugged all the harder. There were all manner of growls and shrieks. The chest bucked and leaped about and finally wrestled younger brother to the ground. Over and over, back and forth, the two of them tumbled. The dust of the road rose up so thick that when it came down, the whole next county was buried.

"Run!" younger brother managed to call out to the others. "Run for your lives. I can't hold it much longer. It's a terrible man-eating Guy-Yookus. Run!"

Felkin leaped for a tree and scooted to the topmost branches. Creel and Huckabuck dug their toes into the ground and took off, skidding about and spewing gravel every which way. How they tore up that ground was a sight to see, for where they went, they left a rut deep enough to bury a cow in.

Younger brother sat up and watched them go. Then he guffawed and chortled and giggled. Afterwards he went to the tree where the horse sat. "Felkin, I 'spect we've seen the last of those twins," he said. "Come on down, and we'll eat a meal of Guy-Yookus."

He helped Felkin down and led him to the chest. He

76

opened it up, and to his delight there was a loaf of fresh bread and a little jar of sourwood honey. There was also a round cheese and a bottle of clear apple cider. They sat right in the middle of the road and feasted. And when they'd eaten and drunk it all and reached the bottom of the chest, there lay a little bag of gold coins.

"Now in the morning we must see if we can find the owner of this fine chest and these gold coins," said younger brother. "He'll hardly begrudge us this food, I reckon, and we can pay him for it by doing a little plowing and planting. But the chest and gold he must have back."

So they curled up by the wayside and slept soundly. Next morning they looked the chest over carefully, and there was the owner's name printed on it plainly. Right next to the lock in little gold letters it said: PAT. PENDING.

"We'll just go a-hunting him," cried younger brother,

and he picked up the chest and started off for town. The first ten people they met had never heard of Mr. Pat Period Pending. But the next man they met said, "Yes, indeed. I've heard of him."

"Do you know him when you see him?" asked younger brother.

"I might," said the man, "if I looked careful."

"Then come with me," begged younger brother. "And when we find him, you'll know him, for I'm not sure I would recognize him a-tall."

They went all about and about and around and about and looked at everybody. But the man said none of the people they saw was Pat. Pending. At last they had looked at the whole population, and younger brother was feeling very discouraged.

"Why, now," cried the man, "you are the onliest one I haven't seen. You must be Pat. Pending yourself under that sack."

Younger brother was afraid to take off the sack. He didn't want to scare folks. Yet the more he thought about it, the more he believed it must be so, for there was a name running around without a person and here he was running around without a name. They must belong to one another. There was only one way to find out, but he didn't dare.

"But I don't want to harm anybody," he said sadly to the man. "I wouldn't want my ugliness to hurt even one person."

"Tell you what," replied the man. "It may be you're not as ugly as you think, for your brothers have been fooling you about many things. It may just be that they have fooled you about this too."

Younger brother shook his head. He thought it might be so, and then again he reckoned it might surely not.

"This is what we'll do," said the man. "You take off the sack, but don't take it off all at once. Take it off a little bit at a time. Every day I'll look at a little more, and that way the shock won't be so great and I'll soon know whether you are Pat. Pending."

So every day younger brother took off a little more of the sack. And every day the man took doses of tonics and strengthening exercises so he would have the strength to look. At the end of a week, younger brother had the sack all the way off.

The man didn't scream. He didn't spot up all blue and green. He didn't melt nor did his innards uncurl and turn to water. Instead, he exclaimed, "Why, you are Mister Pat. Pending. I'd have knowed you anywhere."

Pat. Pending ran to look in the mirror. And right away he recognized himself. He was surprised he hadn't done it long ago.

Then he and Felkin bought themselves a farm and put his name on the mailbox and lived there long and happily with the very best of everything.

79

And was Pat. Pending really so ugly? Well, he was as ugly as most and not so handsome as some, for beauty is only skin deep, they say. And if you have a kind heart and a good head and a willing hand, the way Pat. Pending did, it don't much matter what kind of face you have, now does it?